Finding a Place: Italian Migration to Australia

Carmel Reilly

NELSON
CENGAGE Learning™

Australia • Brazil • Japan • Korea • Mexico • Singapore • Spain • United Kingdom • United States

Finding a Place: Italian Migration to Australia

Fast Forward
Gold Level 22

Text: Carmel Reilly
Editor: Cameron Macintosh
Design: Stella Vassiliou
Series design: James Lowe
Production controller: Seona Galbally
Photo research: Michelle Cottrill
Audio recordings: Juliet Hill, Picture Start
Spoken by: Matthew King and Abbe Holmes
Reprint: Jennifer Foo

Acknowledgements
The author and publisher would like to acknowledge permission to reproduce material from the following sources: Photographs by Fairfax Photos/ Craig Abraham, p15/Nick Moir, p22; Getty Images/David Lees, pp 3, 6; Joseph Shipp, front cover top, pp 1 top, 16, 19; Jupitar Images, pp 20-21; Masterfile, p14; National Archives of Australia, front cover bottom, pp 1 bottom, 4, 5, 7, 8, 10, 11, 13; National Library of Australia/Damian McDonald, p23 right/ J A Mulligan, p17/ Jeff Carter, back cover, p12/ Viscopy/ Wolfgang Seivers, p11 bottom; Newspix/Shannon Morris, p23 left; Photolibrary/Alison Miksch, p9/ Superstock, p18; Queensland Digital Library/John Oxley Library, p11 top.

ISBN 978 0 17 012688 5
ISBN 978 0 17 012681 6 (set)

Cengage Learning Australia
Level 7, 80 Dorcas Street
South Melbourne, Victoria Australia 3205
Phone: 1300 790 853

Cengage Learning New Zealand
Unit 4B Rosedale Office Park
331 Rosedale Road, Albany, North Shore NZ 0632
Phone: 0508 635 766

For learning solutions, visit cengage.com.au

Printed in Australia by Ligare Pty Ltd
5 6 7 8 9 10 11 21 20 19 18 17

Evaluated in independent research by staff from the Department of Language, Literacy and Arts Education at the University of Melbourne.

Finding a Place: Italian Migration to Australia

Carmel Reilly

Contents

ITALIANS IN AUSTRALIA

Italians began **migrating** to Australia in the 1800s, but it wasn't until after the Second World War that they arrived in large numbers.
In the 1950s and 1960s, hundreds of thousands of Italians left Italy to find work and escape poverty.

This was often a very difficult choice for these people to make.
Many families were unable to migrate at the same time.
Sometimes it took years before the whole family was able to meet in Australia.

During this period, more than 250 000 Italian migrants came to Australia. This made Italians the largest non-English-speaking migrant group ever to have arrived on Australian shores.

Chapter 2

ARRIVING

Italians who arrived in Australia after the Second World War found themselves in a very different culture from their own.

Family Life

Family life in Australia was different from family life in Italy.
In Italy, many people lived with extended families in small communities where everybody knew everybody else.
Usually, people felt connected to the local area where they lived.

Australians, however, were more likely to live in nuclear families and to move from place to place.

Language

Australia was an English-speaking country, and most Italians didn't speak English when they arrived.
This made life very difficult for them. Everything from going shopping to finding a job was a challenge for people who didn't have enough English to make themselves understood.

Italian migrants learning English, in 1955

Running Words 224

common Italian foods

Food

Food was always a very important part of Italian culture. However, Italian migrants to Australia in the 1950s were unable to find many familiar foods.

Olive oil could only be bought from a chemist shop. Garlic, pasta, herbs and many fruits and vegetables used in Italy were not available in Australia.

Even Australian bread and cheese was different from the kinds of bread and cheese available in Italy.

DIFFICULT YEARS

Life wasn't easy for Italians in the early years of their migration to Australia.

Language and cultural differences made it difficult for Italians and English-speaking Australians to get to know and understand each other. Furthermore, many Australians found it hard to accept Italians because Italy had been Australia's enemy in the Second World War.

Italian workers arrive in Cairns, 1956, to work on a sugar farm.

Life was also physically hard for Italian migrants. Many new arrivals worked on large construction projects, on farms, or in factories where they had to work hard for low pay.

But they were not afraid of hard work, because they wanted to give their children a better future.

Chapter 4

SETTLING IN

Communities

After a few years, Italian migrants began to settle into life in Australia.

In many places, families bought houses near to each other and formed small Italian communities within suburbs or areas.

People were able to keep their Italian identity within these communities.

They felt free to speak Italian and to carry on many of the old traditions that had always been such a large part of their lives.

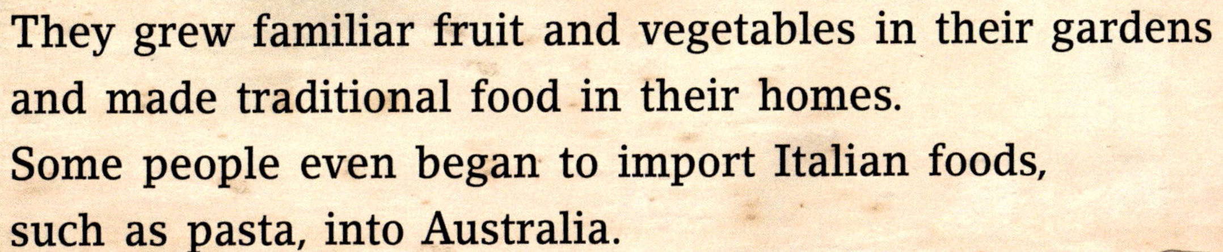

They grew familiar fruit and vegetables in their gardens and made traditional food in their homes.
Some people even began to import Italian foods, such as pasta, into Australia.

Chapter 5

CHANGES

As the years went by, the Italian community started to find its place in Australia.
One of the main reasons for this was the birth of a second **generation**.
The children of migrants grew up as Australians, speaking English –
yet still a part of the migrant Italian culture as well.

Then, in the 1970s, the government of Australia brought in a policy of multiculturalism.

This meant that different ethnic and cultural identities within the community were no longer seen as outside Australian culture (as some people had once believed), but instead were understood to be a part of Australian culture.

At this time, governments also set up special services to make life easier for new migrants.

Chapter 6

A CASE STUDY: FINDING AN IDENTITY

Luisa's family came from Italy in the 1950s. She was born in Melbourne soon after her family arrived.

Her father worked for a construction company, building houses in the suburbs. Until Luisa was born, her mother worked in a factory, making clothes for women.

Luisa, at the age of 9

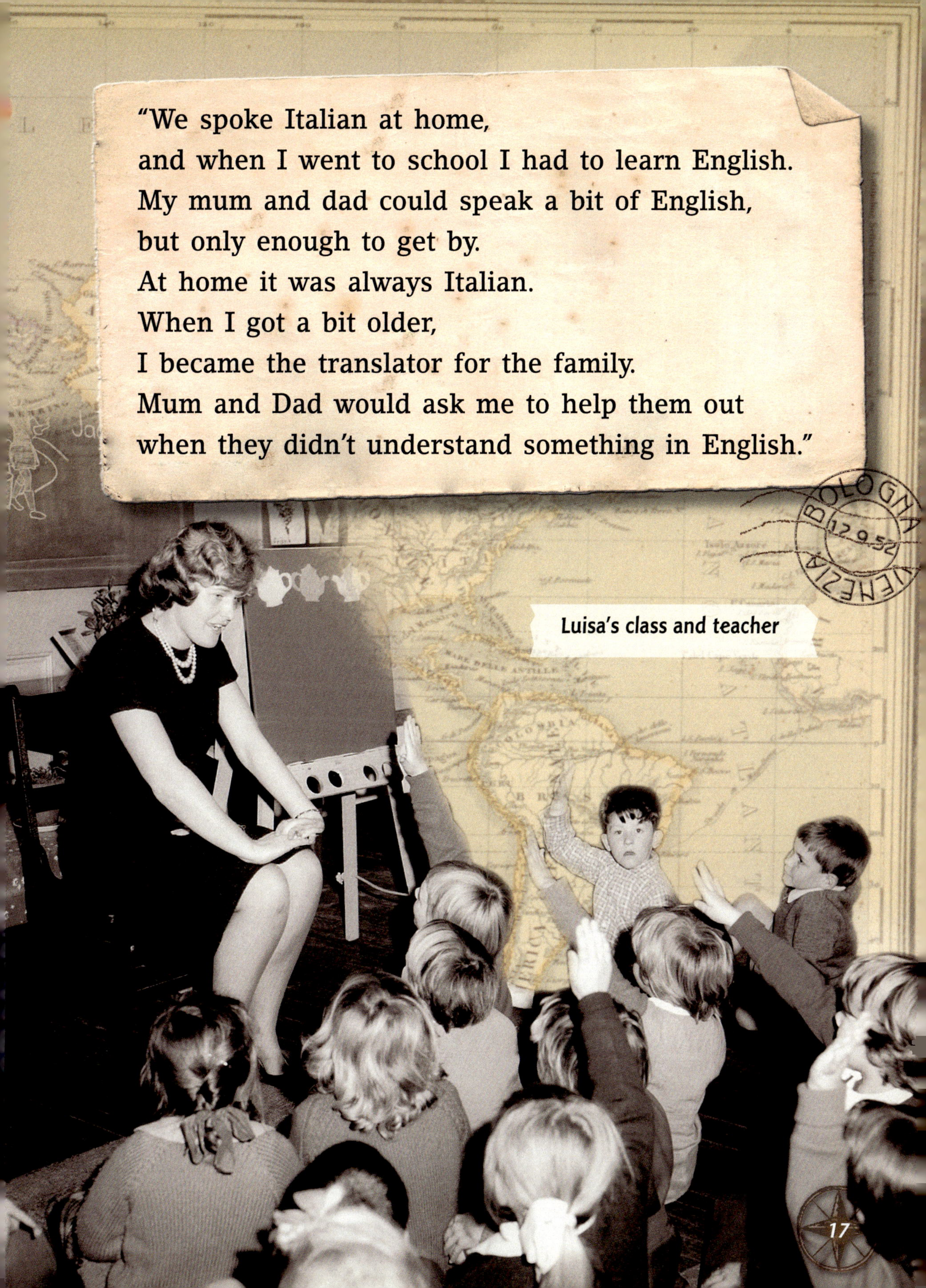

"We spoke Italian at home,
and when I went to school I had to learn English.
My mum and dad could speak a bit of English,
but only enough to get by.
At home it was always Italian.
When I got a bit older,
I became the translator for the family.
Mum and Dad would ask me to help them out
when they didn't understand something in English."

Luisa's class and teacher

“When I was growing up,
my parents were very protective.
I wasn’t allowed to do as much
as some of my Australian friends.
Some of them couldn’t understand
why I couldn’t go out and do things with them,
or why I always did what my parents wanted!

helping Mum with the washing

Luisa aged 16 (far right) with her friends

My family spent a lot of time with other Italians, mainly because it was much easier for my parents to communicate in Italian.
Because of this, I ended up spending more time with kids from Italian backgrounds."

Things have changed now that Luisa has children of her own.
"I'm not as strict as my parents were, so my own kids have more freedom. They can move between the different cultures and feel more at home in both.

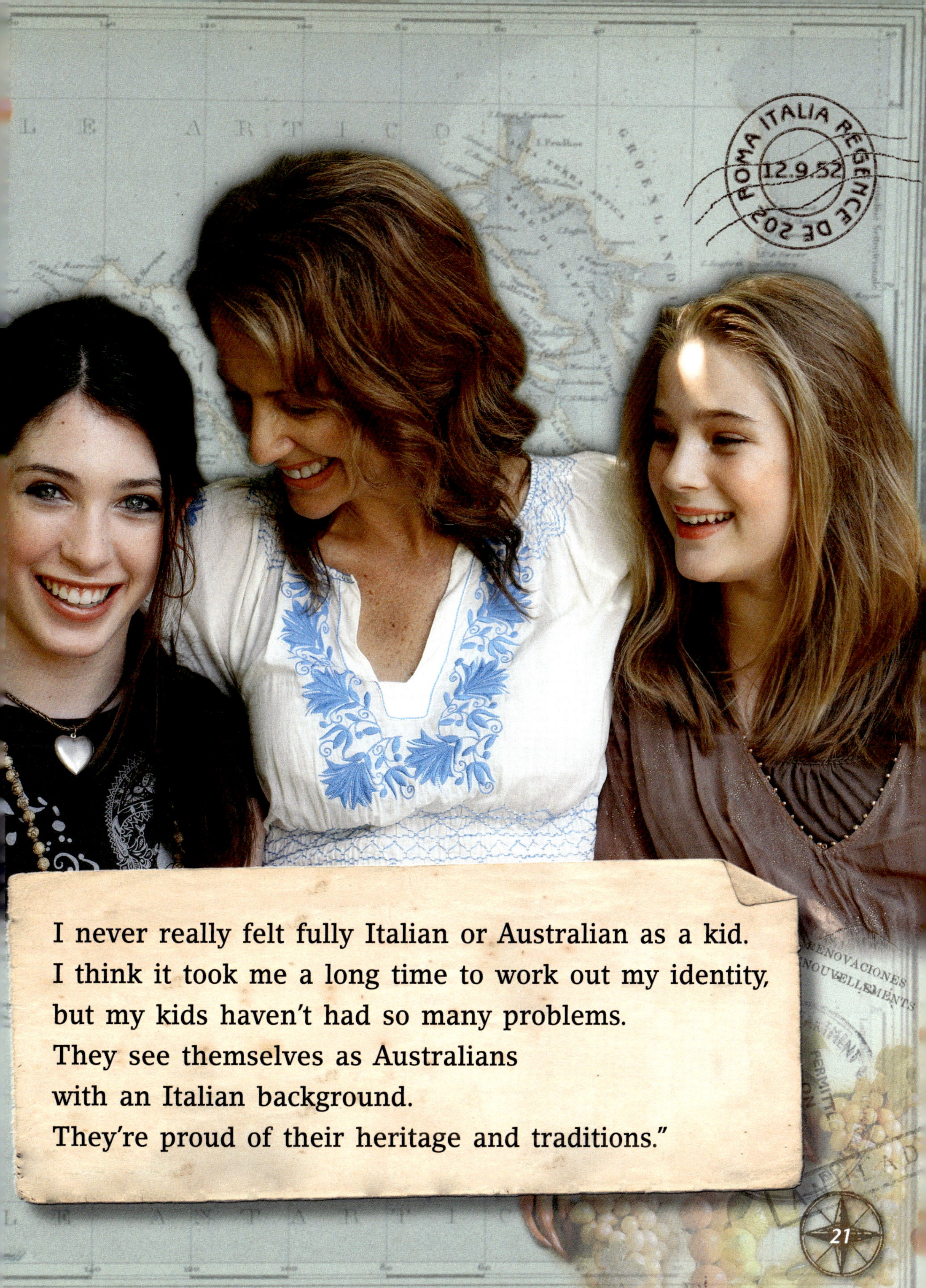

I never really felt fully Italian or Australian as a kid.
I think it took me a long time to work out my identity,
but my kids haven't had so many problems.
They see themselves as Australians
with an Italian background.
They're proud of their heritage and traditions."

"Today, the influence of Italian culture is visible in many areas of Australian life, nowhere more than in the food people eat. Australian food is very influenced by Italian food.
When we go out now, Italian food is everywhere, and many Australians cook Italian foods at home. Everyone drinks Italian-style coffee.

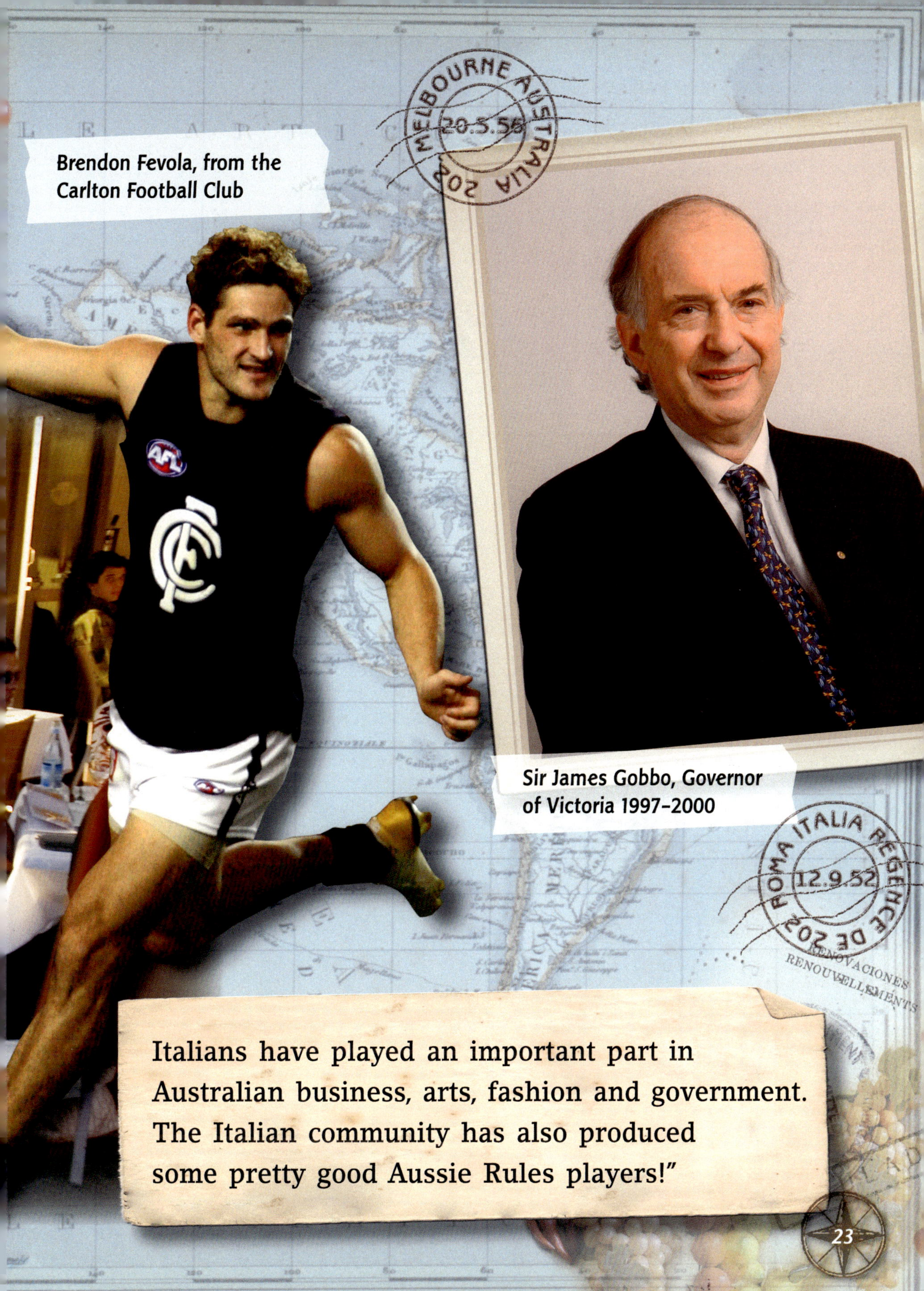

Brendon Fevola, from the Carlton Football Club

Sir James Gobbo, Governor of Victoria 1997–2000

Italians have played an important part in Australian business, arts, fashion and government. The Italian community has also produced some pretty good Aussie Rules players!"

Glossary

generation all the people born at a particular time

migrating moving permanently from one country to another

Index